SURPRISE!
LOOK WHO'S
DOWN THERE

by Gloria Nussbaum
Illustrated by Wendy Matzke

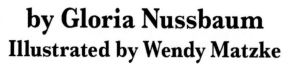

AuthorHouse™
1663 Liberty Drive
Bloomington, IN 47403
www.authorhouse.com
Phone: 1 (800) 839-8640

Published by AuthorHouse 3/25/2015

ISBN: 978-1-4259-8882-1 (sc)
ISBN: 978-1-4969-7176-0 (hc)
ISBN: 978-1-5049-0359-2 (e)

Library of Congress Control Number: 2007901508

Print information available on the last page.

Any people depicted in stock imagery provided by Thinkstock are models, and such images are being used for illustrative purposes only. Certain stock imagery © Thinkstock.

This book is printed on acid-free paper.

Dedication:

To children and all others who use their imagination for the fun of it

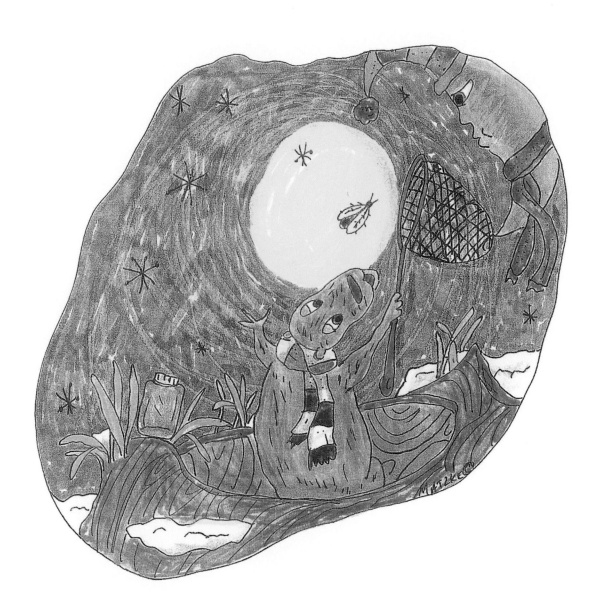

I saw a round brown head rise up

From a round brown hole.

He had round brown eyes. Did you guess?

Yes! It was a mole.

When he saw me and I saw him,

He ducked back down in his hole again.

I wish I could see what it's like down there.

Is a stick his table and a stone his chair?

Does he sleep on moss? Is his bed hard or soft?

Would he let me visit if I could?

Or chase me away as maybe he should

Since people don't welcome him in their yard;

Men, cats and dogs make his life very hard.

What will he do when the rain comes down?

With a hole for a roof, is he going to drown?

Could he plug that hole with a rubber ball,

Or want to have his own waterfall

Right in the middle of his own little room

to shower and play in by the light of the moon?

And when it's very cold outside,

Could he catch a passing firefly

And bring him in to warm his den

And also to light a candle by?

And then when he's sleepy, will he dream

Of a field of flowers next to a stream

Where he plays all day long

And sings a little song?

"See me, find me, look down a round hole, I live there be-cause I'm Mo-ry the Mole"

Tune of "Twinkle, Twinkle, Little Star"

And when he's hungry will he search for food?

Stealing from others would be very rude.

Will the birds be willing to share their seed?

If the feeder is full it's more than they need.

And if he's feeling lonely and sad,

And wishing a friend is what he had,

Could he use his feet as a kind of shovel,

And dig his way to a nearby tunnel?

And when he came up out of the ground,

many new animal friends would be found.

Squirrel, frog, rabbit and skunk,

Blue jay, grey mouse, red robin and chipmunk.

Maybe he would meet sweet Molly McMole,

And invite her home to share his hole.

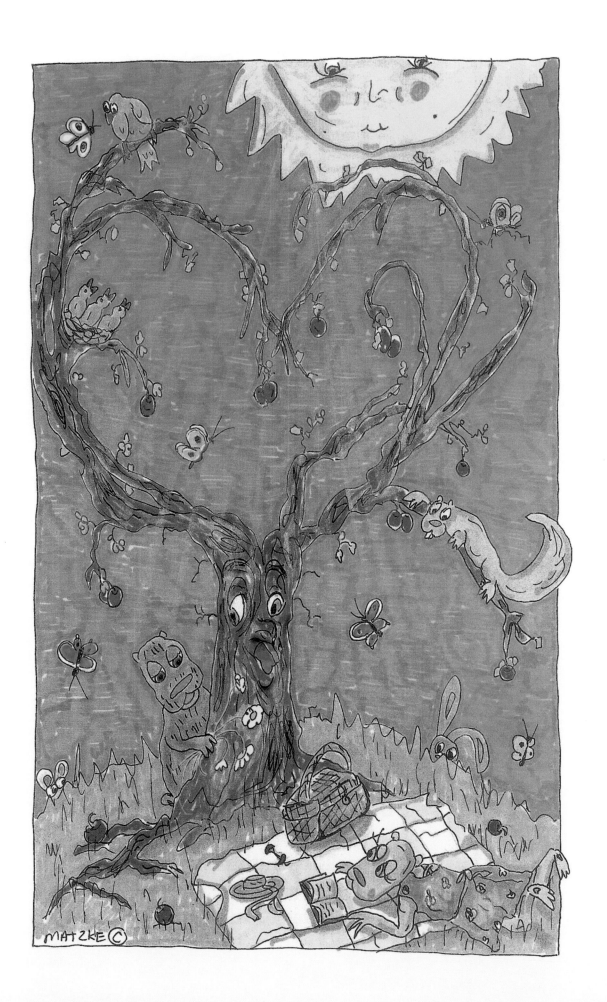

And a wedding would follow in the old rabbit hollow

Of two moles named Molly and Mory,

And there happily ends this partly-true story.

Did this really happen; could it be true?

Well, believe me when I tell you

That I went back to find the grassy knoll

Where I first saw that round brown hole...

And up popped TWO heads from that very SAME hole,

I'm sure it was Mory and Molly McMole.

And then I saw him give me a wink.

So now you tell me, what do you think?

Printed in the United States
by Baker & Taylor Publisher Services